BEAR'S BIRTHDAY

Written by Stella Blackstone
Illustrated by Debbie Harter

Bear has blown up ten big balloons.
His party guests will be here soon!

10

Bear opens the door to welcome his friends.
He's hoping his day of fun never ends.

9

The first game they play is
hide-and-seek. Where is Bear?
Can you see his feet?

8

Next they all play musical chairs.
There's not enough room for so many bears.

7

The group hunts for treasure
among the trees.
Bear crouches down:
guess what he sees!

Bear unwraps the treasure and looks inside.
He has a wonderful birthday surprise!

5

It's full of delicious jam and honey:
Raspberry, strawberry, apricot, cherry.

4

The table is covered with tasty treats.
It's time for Bear's big birthday feast!

WITHDRAWN